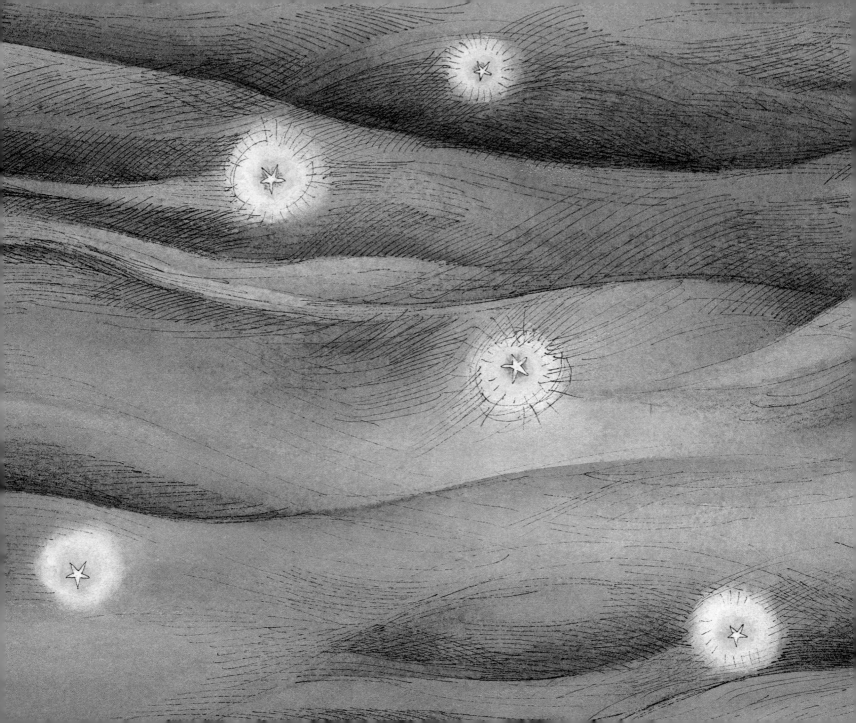

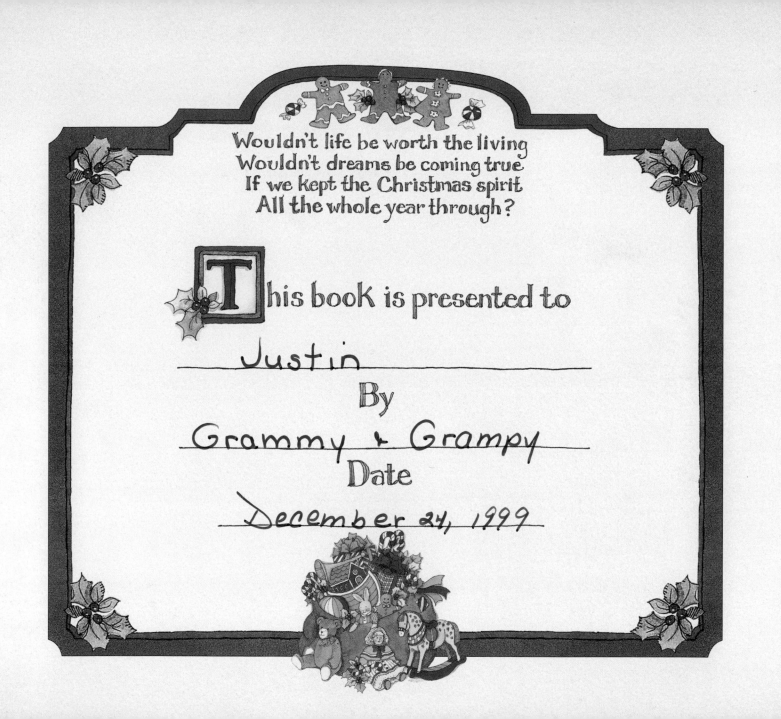

Wouldn't life be worth the living
Wouldn't dreams be coming true
If we kept the Christmas spirit
All the whole year through?

This book is presented to

Justin

By

Grammy & Grampy

Date

December 24, 1999

Text by Clement Clarke Moore
Illustrations by Susan Winget
Copyright 1999 All rights reserved

Published by   10 9 8 7 6 5 4 3 2 1
Lang Books   ISBN. 0-7412-0285-9

A Division of
R.A. Lang Card Co. Ltd.
514 Wells Street
Delafield, WI 53018

In the winter of 1822, Clement Clarke Moore affectionately laid down the words of this poem as a holiday gift for his six children. As they gathered around him by the fireside in the family mansion in New York City, they listened with wide-eyed wonder while their father described the approaching visit from St. Nicholas.

Although the legend of St. Nicholas had its beginning with a fourth-century Byzantine Bishop, who was a staunch protector of the Christian faith, over the years he was mystically transformed into colorful figures who reflected traditions and popular culture of that time. In England, he was known as Father Christmas, in Holland as Sinter Klaas, in France the children called him Pere Noel and in Germany, Weinachtsman.

Clement Moore's St. Nicholas was based on a Dutch tale he remembered from his childhood. His creation of a jolly old elf, fashioned after a Dutch caretaker that had worked on the family estate, has become a much loved universal symbol of generosity and good will. Throughout the years this delightful poem has enamoured children and adults alike as they share a rich heritage of family traditions during the holiday season.

Our warmest wish is that this book, through Clement Moore's magical words and Susan Winget's charming illustrations, will bring to life the simple pleasures of childhood... the joy of anticipation and the thrill of the imagination. As you share "The Night Before Christmas" with family and friends may you create priceless memories and cherished traditions that will grow richer with the passing of time.

SAWinget ©1996

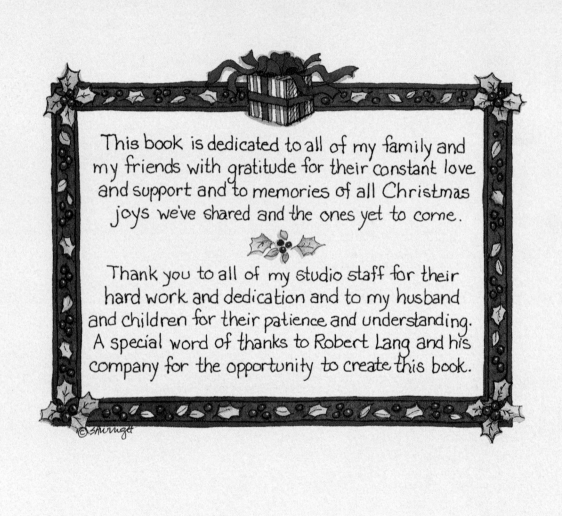

This book is dedicated to all of my family and my friends with gratitude for their constant love and support and to memories of all Christmas joys we've shared and the ones yet to come.

Thank you to all of my studio staff for their hard work and dedication and to my husband and children for their patience and understanding. A special word of thanks to Robert Lang and his company for the opportunity to create this book.

THE NIGHT BEFORE CHRISTMAS

CLEMENT C. MOORE

· illustrated by Susan Winget ·

'Twas the night before Christmas when all through the house, not a creature was stirring...

. . . not even a mouse.

The stockings were hung by the chimney with care, in hopes that St. Nicholas...

...soon would be there.

Dear Santa We have been so good this year.

The children were nestled all snug in their beds, While visions of sugar-plums danced in their heads.

And mamma
in her kerchief,
and I in my cap...

Had just settled down for a long winter's nap.

When out on the lawn there arose such a clatter, I sprang from my bed to see what was the matter.

Away to the window I flew like a flash, tore open the shutters and threw up the sash.

The moon on the breast of the new-fallen snow, gave a lustre of midday to objects below; when what to my wondering eyes should appear but a miniature sleigh and eight tiny reindeer, with a little old driver, so lively and quick, I knew in a moment it must be St. Nick! More rapid than eagles his coursers they came, and he whistled and shouted and called them by name.

"Now, Dasher! now, Dancer! now, Prancer and Vixen!
On, Comet! on, Cupid! on, Donder and Blitzen!

To the top of the porch, to the top of the wall,

Now, dash away, dash away, dash away all!"

As dry leaves that before the wild hurricane fly,
when they meet with an obstacle
mount to the sky,
So, up to the housetop the coursers they flew,
with a sleigh full of toys
and St. Nicholas, too.

And then, in a twinkling, I heard on the roof, the prancing and pawing of each little hoof.

As I drew in
my head

and was
turning around,

Down the chimney
St. Nicholas came with a bound.

He was dressed all in fur from his head to his foot,
and his clothes were all tarnished with ashes and soot.

A bundle of toys he had flung on his back, and he looked like a peddler just opening his pack.

His droll little mouth was drawn up like a bow, and the beard on his chin was as white as the snow. The stump of a pipe he held tight in his teeth, And the smoke, it encircled his head like a wreath.

He had a broad face and a little round belly that shook when he laughed, like a bowl full of jelly.

He was chubby and plump,
a right jolly old elf;
and I laughed when
I saw him, in spite
of myself;

A wink of his eye, and
a twist of his head,
soon gave me to know
I had nothing
to dread.

He spoke not a word,
but went straight to his work,
and filled all the stockings,
then turned with a jerk...

And laying his finger aside of his nose,
and giving a nod, up the
chimney he rose.

And away they all flew

Like the down of a thistle.

But I heard him exclaim,
Ere he drove out of sight.

"Happy Christmas
to all, and to all a
good-night!"

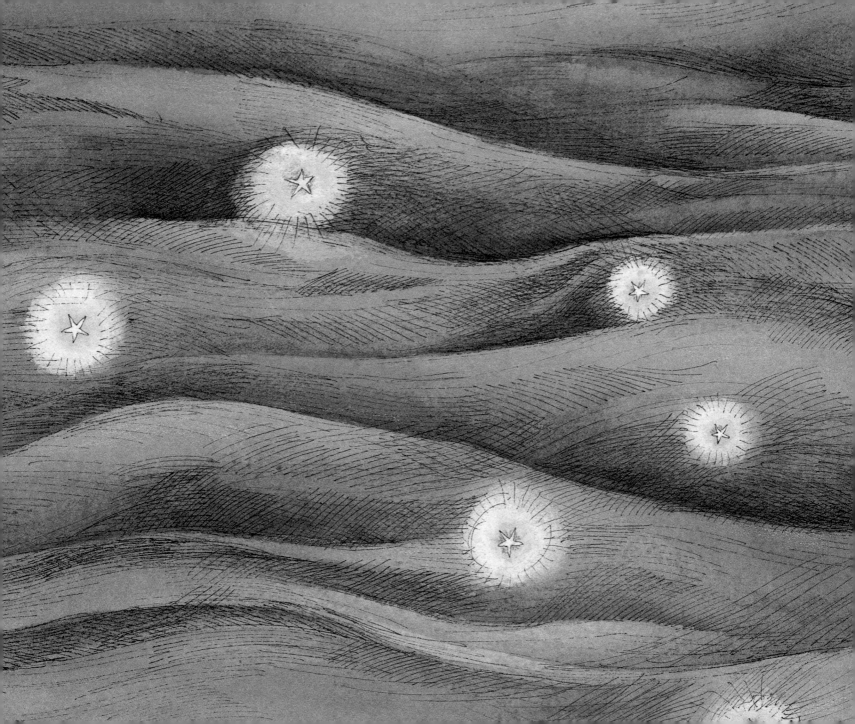